Stepney

Orinoco

WOMBLES™

This book belongs to

Ethan..............................

My favourite Womble is

Tomsk..............................

Stories by Elisabeth Beresford
Additional material by Graham Wise and Geoff Cowans
Illustrations by Alan Willow and Mark Ripley
Design by Hilary Edwards-Malam

Wombles created by Elisabeth Beresford

The Wombles™
© Elisabeth Beresford/FilmFair Ltd. 1998
Licensed by Copyrights
Published in Great Britain in 1998 by World International Ltd.,
Deanway Technology Centre, Wilmslow Road, Handforth, Cheshire SK9 3FB

Printed in Italy   ISBN 0 7498 3798 5

£5.50
UK ONLY

CONTENTS

BUNGO FLIES HIGH

"It was a warm, windy sort of day on Wimbledon Common. Sort of windy because the short, sharp gusts kept blowing rubbish all over the place. Then the wind would go away leaving rubbish everywhere.

"Oh dear! How can a Womble clean up the Common on a day like this?" grumbled Bungo, hanging on to his Tidy Bag. "I ask you!"

And at that moment the wind howled again and Bungo had to hold on to his cap to stop it blowing away. Then he spotted some string lying in the grass.

"Perhaps I could tie things down with that string!" said Bungo.

He pushed his Tidy Bag into an old tree stump to keep it safe.

"Now I've got both paws free to roll up that string," said Bungo, starting to feel rather pleased with himself.

But the string was longer than he thought it would be. He followed it on and on and on until at last he reached the end… and there was a kite caught in a bush.

"Wait until the others see this!" said Bungo.

But at that moment there was another very strong gust of wind. It lifted the kite up into the sky and Bungo went with it!

"Owwww!" shouted Bungo.

Wellington, who was tidying up down below on the Common, nearly jumped out of his fur.

"What are you doing up there, Bungo?" he called out.

Bungo was in too much of a panic to answer. Supposing he got blown all the way up to Scotland and landed on the MacWomble's burrow! But then the wind dropped. And so did the kite! Down and down it went until it landed in the top of a tree. Bungo made a grab for a branch and the kite fluttered to the ground.

"Get me down!" shouted Bungo, with his eyes tightly shut.

"I'll try to think of a way. Just hold on," said Wellington, going round and round in circles. And then a spider's web caught his eye.

"Perhaps I could make a sort of net to catch Bungo," Wellington muttered to himself. Wellington's mutterings were heard by Obidos. Obidos's home is in a burrow far away in Brazil, and he hadn't been on Wimbledon Common for long.

Obidos had never seen a Womble trapped at the top of a tree before. While Wellington was still thinking things over, Obidos trotted back to the burrow to see what help he could find. Obidos burst through the front door and almost tripped over a long, wide ribbon of paper that was being pumped out of a machine. There was a great deal of whirrings, pingings and bleeps. It was the Wom-Fax and Great Uncle Bulgaria was standing watching it.

"Quite splendid!" he said. "This amazing machine can send and receive messages from Wombles all over the world!"

"Not bad at all," said Tobermory – who had invented the Wom-Fax, but didn't want to make a lot of fuss about it. "It gives us a lot of extra paper too. We could turn it into wallpaper."

Obidos jumped over the paper and told the two Wombles about Bungo being stuck at the top of a tree.

"Goodness gracious me!" said Great Uncle Bulgaria. "You need a net to catch Bungo in? But I don't know where…"

"I've got a better idea," said Tobermory, scooping up a great roll of fax paper. He fetched an old belt from his workshop. He stapled it to the paper and then doubled the paper over and glued it together to make it extra strong.

"Lead on, Obidos," said Tobermory. "There's not a moment to lose!"

"Ooooh I feel so dizzy," wailed poor Bungo, hanging on to the tree for dear life. It was swaying backwards and forwards in the wind and he was starting to feel tree sick. "Where's the net, Wellington?"

"Sorry," said Wellington, polishing his spectacles. "I'm still sort of working out how to make it and … hold on there's someone coming!"

Both the young Wombles were very glad to see Great Uncle Bulgaria, Tobermory and Obidos hurrying towards them.

"Now then young Bungo, I'll throw this up to you," Tobermory called out.

"I don't think I want anything up here," said poor Bungo. "I want to come down there with you!"

"In a minute," said Tobermory. "All you've got to do is use this!"

The fax paper had been folded into a neat bundle with the belt strapped round it. Tobermory threw it up and Bungo caught it – just.

"Open out the paper, hang on to the belt and let go of the branch," Tobermory said firmly.

"I'll fall," wailed Bungo.

"You'll float!" said Tobermory even more firmly.

Bungo took a deep breath, closed his eyes tightly and jumped off the tree top, clinging to the belt with all his might. It was like a handle and above his head the paper unfolded and turned into a parachute. Blowing from side to side it very gently landed Bungo on the ground. He was so surprised, and so delighted, he could hardly speak for a moment. Most unlike Bungo. But he managed it.

"Thanks, Tobermory," said Bungo. "I say, can I have another go? That was good fun. Like flying. I could be the first flying Womble!"

"Better not risk it, in case the paper tears," said Tobermory.

"Tears!" said Bungo. His back paws suddenly went all weak and wobbly. "Tears! I never thought of that…"

Suddenly the wind began to blow again. Tobermory folded up the parachute before it could get blown away and Bungo collected his Tidy Bag.

"Back to the burrow for tea," said Great Uncle Bulgaria. "And as for you young Bungo, I think you'd better keep your back paws firmly on the ground for a bit!

Make a WOM-CHUTE

"Young Bungo had quite an adventure! I was rather pleased with my idea for getting him down from that tree. If you'd like, you can make a Wom-Chute of your very own. Just follow these instructions."

You will need:
One piece of A4 white paper
Cotton
Safety scissors
A ruler
A pencil
A small plate
Sticky tape
A large paper clip

1 Put the plate face down on the piece of paper. Draw round it with your pencil.

2 Ask an adult to use the scissors to cut out the circle you've drawn.

3 Ask an adult to cut four pieces of cotton which are all the same length (25cm).

25cm

4 Use sticky tape to attach the end of one piece of cotton to the edge of your paper circle.

5 Repeat this with the other three pieces of cotton.

Now your Wom-Chute is ready to use. Hold it up as high as you can, then let go and watch it float down.

6 Take one of the loose cotton ends and tie it around one end of the paper clip. Then do the same with each of the other three loose ends of cotton.

Things that go WHOOSH in the Night...

1 Late one night Tomsk suddenly woke up. "Hmm," he thought, "how can I make myself fall asleep again?" First he tried staring at the ceiling. Then he closed his eyes and tried counting sheep. But it wasn't long before he gave up. Counting sheep was far too difficult!

2 Tomsk lay on his stomach. But still he couldn't sleep.

3 He twisted one way, then another. He twisted and turned back again.

4 Then he lay on his left side. And then on his right. But not for long...

5 "I'm still not sleepy!" said Tomsk. "Perhaps a nice, warm drink will help." He got out of bed and headed for Madame Cholet's kitchen. A hot cup of dandelion tea usually made him feel sleepy.

6 Great Uncle Bulgaria woke up too. He heard strange noises coming from outside his bedroom door.
Bang! Clang! Smash! Crash! And, after that and loudest of all, "Waaaaaah!"

7 The strange noises woke Tobermory too!

8 And they woke Obidos in his bedroom.

9 They even woke Alderney in her treehouse.

10 And so, because Wombles can't help being curious, they all got out of their beds to see just what was making all the noise.

11 "Good gracious!" exclaimed Great Uncle Bulgaria. "Oh, my!" cried Madame Cholet. The sounds they heard were made by Tomsk as he shot through the burrow in a blur. "Help!" he cried as he whizzed round a corner.

12 "What on earth is going on?" asked Stepney, as he stumbled from his bedroom. "Something very strange is happening to young Tomsk," mused Great Uncle Bulgaria.

13 "Help!" cried Tomsk as he rocketed past them. "I think," decided Great Uncle Bulgaria, "we had better try to slow him down." "Or no one will get back to sleep tonight!" yawned Orinoco.

14 "Leave this to me," said Stepney. "I know how to solve this little problem, but I need you all to help. Go and get your bedclothes!" The Wombles all disappeared back into their bedrooms.

15 Stepney dashed off. He soon reappeared dragging the blanket and pillows from his bed.

16 The Wombles made a huge, soft barrier. It stretched right across the corridor.

17 "Arrrrgh!" cried Tomsk, as he crashed into the Wom-Barrier. He lay in a tangled heap on the floor.

18 "Tomsk, what are those on your feet?" asked Alderney. "I don't know," replied Tomsk. "I stepped into them in the dark."

19 "Ooops!" said Orinoco. "I found them on the Common. I must have dropped them!" "Well, you can have them back now," said Tomsk. "I'm ready to go back to bed." "Not so fast," chuckled Alderney. "Now it's my turn to have some fun with those wheelie good shoes!"

SHANSI'S SECRET GARDEN

Shansi is a rather shy, small Womble who has come all the way from China to stay with the Wombles of Wimbledon Common. Everybody was very kind to her. Great Uncle Bulgaria told her stories about the days when he was a young Womble – so long ago that hardly anybody could imagine it. Tobermory showed her around the Workshop, and Wellington showed her how some of the machines worked. Madame Cholet made her special rice daisy buns. Alderney took her up to her treehouse and Tomsk said she could go jogging with him. Stepney let her push his barrow, Bungo carried her Tidy Bag for her when it got very heavy, and Orinoco even offered her a share of his bracken and buttercup sandwich!

But Shansi still felt quite shy.

"What she needs is a special little place all of her own," said Great Uncle Bulgaria.

"A Shansi store cupboard in my kitchen?" asked Madame Cholet.

"Not quite," said Great Uncle Bulgaria.

"A bench in my Workshop?" asked Tobermory. "She's very neat with her paws."

"Nearly there," said Great Uncle Bulgaria. "I know! Her own little bit of the Common which will make her feel at home. A kind of Secret Garden!" he said.

All the other Wombles were told about the idea. They were not to tell Shansi. Every time they were out on the Common they kept their eyes open looking for the perfect place for her. It was Alderney who came up with the perfect place.

It happened one evening when she was up in her treehouse watching the sun go down.

It was a very red sun and it turned the water of Queen's Mere – a big pond which Alderney kept clear of rubbish – a pretty pink colour. And then, just before the sun set, Alderney saw a small bit of Common surrounded by water and reeds. She had never noticed it before and she knew at once it would make a lovely Secret Garden for Shansi.

"Perfect!" said Great Uncle Bulgaria.

"Oh oh oh oh!" said Shansi, who was so happy she couldn't think of anything to say at all.

Every day after she finished work Shansi trotted off to her Secret Garden, and soon she was growing a special water weed and then some water flowers and blossom. It made her think of the Womble Burrow back in China.

There was only one thing that worried her. How could she say 'thank you' to all the Wimbledon Wombles? And then one day, just as she and Alderney and Wellington were finishing tidying up work, Wellington spotted an enormous, battered box which some untidy Human Being had dumped really close to Shansi's Secret Garden.

"Just look at that!" said Wellington. "It's full of boots!"

"Even Tobermory couldn't make them into anything," said Alderney.

Shansi didn't say anything at all. She just stared and stared at all the different boots. She was having a wonderful idea! She knew just how she could make her Secret Garden special for all the other Wombles. What she did was to turn the boots into very special flower pots. In some of them she grew beautiful flowers for Great Uncle Bulgaria's study, Tobermory's Workshop and Madame Cholet's kitchen. In the others she grew fruit and vegetable and salad plants, because she knew the young Wombles are always hungry and they really enjoy trying out tasty new food.

"I think your food is bootiful," said Tomsk. Everybody laughed.

But Orinoco got the biggest laugh when he finished his third plate of Water Weed and Blossom soup and said: "I say Shansi – if we made you an even bigger Secret Garden you could grow even more food! Is there any of that Cherry Reed cake left, Madame Cholet?"

"Oh oh oh," said Shansi. And she laughed more than any of them!

There is a good view of the Common from up here! I can see five of my Womble friends below. Can you find their names in this wordsquare?

There is one other name hidden. Can you guess whose name it is? The answers are on page 61.

Obidos

Stepney

Alderney

Tomsk

T	O	M	S	K	C	V	A
G	W	N	H	Q	Z	X	L
M	O	E	A	E	L	M	D
W	B	U	N	G	O	O	E
N	I	K	S	K	I	U	R
Z	D	C	I	B	T	W	N
H	O	M	E	R	Q	P	E
N	S	T	E	P	N	E	Y

Bungo

Orinoco loves munching
juicy strawberries.
How many words can you make out of

STRAWBERRIES

?

TUG·O·MORY

"Oh yes, very useful, if I say so myself," muttered Tobermory as he stood back and admired his latest piece of handiwork.

It was a strange looking machine made up of all kinds of odd bits and pieces. There was a large spring, the insides of an old grandfather clock, some rope, and a sink plunger.

"A clockwork-powered, rope-firing, pulling machine," Tobermory said happily. "It's for pulling out bits of rubbish which have been dumped in ditches and other difficult places. I've only got two problems now. One, will it work? And, two, what shall I call it? Tut tut tut. Very difficult!"

In the kitchen, Madame Cholet had things on her mind too. Like why was Tobermory late for lunch!

"It cannot be that suddenly he doesn't like my cooking," she said crossly. "Why it's moss pie, buttercup crumpets and bramble jelly. And they are delicious!"

"Rather!" agreed Orinoco between mouthfuls. "I tell you what Madame Cholet, if Tobermory doesn't want his I could always eat it for him, you know."

"Now then, young Womble, don't talk with your mouth full," said Great Uncle Bulgaria. "Madame Cholet please don't upset yourself. I'm sure there's a very good reason why Tobermory's late. And it won't have anything to do with your cooking!"

"Oh how kind of you Monsieur Bulgaria," said Madame Cholet. "But what can the trouble be?"

"We can soon find out," said Bungo in his usual bossy way. "We can just ask Tobermory. He's been in the Workshop all morning."

"He was there most of yesterday too," said Tomsk. "I don't know what he's up to. What do you think, Wellington?"

"I think we'd better go and have a look!" said Wellington.

"Very well, off you go if you've finished eating," said Great Uncle Bulgaria, who was longing to know what was going on in the Workshop himself.

"Oui, oui, off with you," said Madame Cholet, getting another plateful of buttercup crumpets out of the oven. "Do 'ave one of these Monsieur Bulgaria. It's a brand new recipe!"

The two young Wombles hurried through the Burrow to the Workshop, their fur standing up in tufts because they wanted to know what was going on! But when they got to the door it wouldn't open. And no wonder because inside the Workshop the handle had just come clean off in Tobermory's paw. It was an old horseshoe and he had meant to put some oil on it for some time.

"Oh drat," muttered Tobermory. "Now what am I going to do! I shall miss my lunch if I don't look out…"

Then he spotted his Voice Trumpet. It was something he had invented some while ago and it was made out of an old road cone. It looked a bit like an enormous ice-cream cornet.

"That's it!" said Tobermory. "I'll call for help."

He picked up the trumpet and put it close to his mouth, took a deep breath and then shouted just as Wellington and Tomsk were putting their ears to the other side of the door to see if they could hear anything.

"HEEEEEELP!" roared Tobermory.

The two young Wombles turned into furry little statues. In fact their fur stood straight on end. It was a truly terrible noise.

Tomsk recovered first.

"Wh-wh-what's that?" he asked.

"It's ME," Tobermory roared back. "Give the door a push. It's stuck and I'm stuck inside. The handle must have jammed the lock!"

They pushed and pushed, but it was no good.

"There must be a way of opening it," said Wellington polishing his spectacles which had misted over.

"Perhaps we could knock it down?" suggested Tomsk.

"Or we could tap on the door hinges," said Wellington. "That might do it..."

Tobermory was working out a plan too. It didn't take him long because he was getting very hungry.

"Of course! Why didn't I think of it before," he said to himself. This will be a chance to try out my clockwork-powered, rope-firing... well, my new invention that I haven't got a name for yet..."

Tobermory did his best to explain his plan to the others, but with a very solid door between them it wasn't easy. He turned the machine towards the door, took careful aim and pulled a lever. There was a loud whirring sound as a spring uncoiled. It fired out one end of the rope. The plunger on the end hit the Workshop door with a THUD!

Outside, Wellington and Tomsk listened nervously.

"Cor! What was THAT?" said Tomsk.

"Are you all right, Tobermory?" called out Wellington.

"So far, so good," Tobermory shouted back. "Now stand well clear."

THUD!

Tobermory leant over and began to wind in the rope. The plunger stuck to the door like glue. There was a great deal of creaking and groaning. Tomsk and Wellington looked at each other and then stood back – just in case. Inside the Workshop Tobermory huffed and puffed as he reeled in the rope as tightly as he could.

"Any minute now," he muttered to himself.

He was right, too. With a CRAAACK the door was pulled clean off its hinges. It crashed down right in front of him.

Wellington was first into the Workshop and in a cloud of dust he saw Tobermory sitting on the floor.

"Are you all right?" he asked anxiously.

"Yes, thank you," said Tobermory getting to his back paws and dusting down his fur. "And what's more, so is my amazing clockwork-powered, rope firing, pulling… er, this machine I've just built!"

CRAAACK

"Splendid!" said Great Uncle Bulgaria, as Tobermory and all the other Wombles sat round the kitchen table having second helpings.

"All's well that ends well," agreed Tobermory, helping himself to another buttercup crumpet. "Pulling down that door was a right little tug of war!"

"More like a Tug-o-Mory. Ha ha ha!" said Tomsk.

Tobermory stopped in mid bite and smiled from ear to ear.

"Well done, young Tomsk," he said. "That's my last problem solved! That's what I'll call my new invention – the Tug-o-Mory!"

STEPNEY and the SNOW WOMBLE

"It's very quiet this morning," thought Stepney rolling over in his nice warm bed. He looked up at the clock on the wall. Yes, the first lot of working Wombles must be out tidying the Common by now. It was funny that he hadn't heard them get up and go for their breakfast. Usually they made quite a lot of noise. In fact, come to think of it, there wasn't a sound anywhere...

Stepney sat up and looked hard at the clock. It was one he had found himself and Wellington had mended it with bits from an old radio so it "tick tocked" rather loudly, but it kept very good time. Stepney held his breath. No, not a voice or a footstep anywhere. His fur began to stand up on end. Nobody had said anything about a change of plans last night, had they?

It had been great fun in the kitchen last night. After two helpings of very nice Bramble Pie, Great Uncle Bulgaria had told them about how Queen's Mere had frozen over when he was a young Womble. They had all gone skating on it. And Tomsk had shown them the sledge he was making out of old bits of wood. And he, Stepney, had offered to help him because he knew all about making things since he had made his own barrow. And then he had told them a few stories about his own home burrow in Stepney and how much more rubbish the Wombles there cleared up than the Wombles of Wimbledon Common...

And quite suddenly sitting up all alone in his quiet little bedroom Stepney realised that last night for some reason he had shown off quite dreadfully in front of everyone. And once he had started he hadn't been able to stop. He remembered Wellington looking down at his plate and Alderney and Shansi nudging each other, and Orinoco had just fallen fast asleep with his head on the table.

"Oh dear!" whispered Stepney to himself. He came as near to blushing as a Womble can. Perhaps they had all gone away and left him because he was such a show-off! Stepney rolled out of his bunk, pulled on his sweater and went out to look for the other Wombles. But the whole Burrow was empty. Nobody in the kitchen, or the Workshop or Great Uncle Bulgaria's study. They had vanished!

"Oh dear, oh dear, OH DEAR!" said Stepney to himself. "Oh please come back everybody. I'll never show off again! I promise!"

But there was not a sound except for the thump-thump-thump of his own back paws running through the Burrow, up to the front door. It stuck for a moment, and then with a CLANG! down came the door and Stepney was out on the Common. And his mouth fell wide open.

He had never seen anything like it before in his whole life. Everything was covered in snow. Thick, white, shining snow which was so bright he couldn't see anything for a moment. And then he saw two small, round figures on a sledge come whizzing down a slope until they hit something and went head over heels. Nearer at hand some other small Wombles were having a tremendous snowball battle and in the far distance he thought he could just make out some rather older Wombles skating on Queen's Mere.

"Oh my!" said Stepney. He thought he heard something behind him and he turned round and came face to face with himself! There he was, a snow Womble wearing a silly great grin on his face and with a Tidy Bag full of snowballs over his arm.

"Hello Stepney," said Wellington, crunching up to him through the snow. "So you've woken up then. We thought we'd let you lie in because you must have been tired after last night when – er, um, ah…"

"When I talked so much," said Stepney. "I'll never, ever show off again. Promise!"

"All this snow makes me think of Madame Cholet's daisy ice-cream," said Orinoco walking up to them to get a snowball. "Bet you don't get snow like this, Stepney!"

"Well, yes. NO!" said Stepney.

"The good thing about it," said Bungo puffing up, "is that the Human Beings don't come out so there's no rubbish. What do you think of the Snow Womble? I made it!"

"Not bad," said Stepney and then, being Stepney, he just could not help himself. "But I think we could make it even better… if you'd care to lend me a paw that is!"

And they did.

Make a WOMBLE TIDY BAG

When the Wombles go tidying on Wimbledon Common, they put all the interesting things they find in a special collecting bag. Here's how to make a Tidy Bag of your own!

You will need:

2 pieces of white A4 thin card
Glue
Ruler
Pencil
Safety scissors
Red felt-tip pen or crayon

1 Take a piece of card and fold it in half so the shorter sides meet.

2 Measure 3cm from each edge along the fold. Draw a dot. Draw a line to join each dot to the corner.

3cm
3cm

3 Ask an adult to cut along the lines.

4 Glue the two cut sides together. Ask an adult to help. Set aside to dry.

5 Take the other card. Measure 3cm from the corner along the short side. Draw a dot. Do the same on the opposite edge. Join the dots.

3cm

6 Ask an adult to cut along this line. This is the bag's handle.

7 Fold the strip of card in half. Stick each end of the strip to the inside of your bag with glue.

Glue

8 Take a red felt-tip pen or crayon and draw a big circle on the bag. Draw a W inside it.

W

Now you can go tidying and collecting like the Wombles.

What interesting things can you find to put in your Tidy Bag?

Madame Cholet's Day Off

1 One morning, as usual, Madame Cholet watched as everyone's cups and saucers, plates, knives, forks and spoons were cleared away after breakfast. But then something very strange happened…

2 Madame Cholet put on her finest clothes and quietly closed the kitchen door.

3 "Monsieur Bulgaria," she said, "today I go for a little walk to inspect the bracken. Perhaps soon we shall have bracken pies!"

4 And off she went. "Don't worry though, for I shall be back in time for supper!" she called happily, as she walked out through the doorway.

5 "Um, is anyone here?" asked Orinoco. "I'm feeling a little hungry!"

6 "Hello, hello, what do we have here?" said Tobermory. "Madame Cholet is missing!" cried Orinoco. "So, I'm going to have a snack."

7 Tobermory was feeling a little hungry too. "It's time for a snack search!" he said.

8 Soon, Wellington Bungo, Tomsk, Obidos, and Shansi were helping too! "Have you lost something?" asked Alderney, as she peeked into the kitchen. "Not my appetite!" replied Orinoco.

9 Before long, Great Uncle Bulgaria arrived to see what was going on. "Where is Madame Cholet?" asked Bungo. Great Uncle Bulgaria sighed, sat down and began to explain. "She'll be back in time for supper," he said.

10 "Supper-time!" wailed Orinoco. "We can't wait that long. We haven't even had lunch yet!"

11 "Hmm," pondered Tobermory. "Then I suppose we'll have to make our own lunch!"

12 Bungo and Orinoco decided to make an icky, sticky, chocolate cake, using Tobermory's brand new invention: the super-stirrer.

13 "Oh, dear!" said Great Uncle Bulgaria, looking at the mess. "Wombles, we'll all be in trouble if Madame Cholet sees her kitchen like this!"

14 So the Wombles tidied up, because that's what Wombles do best!

15 And they finished just in time! "Hello," called Madame Cholet. "Oh, it is so good to be back in my so neat, so tidy kitchen!" "Do you think she knows what happened?" Tomsk whispered to Orinoco. "Well, I won't tell if you won't!"

ALDERNEY the
WATER WOMBLE

'’ve never known weather like it!” said Great Uncle Bulgaria peering out of the front door of the Burrow. He had been looking forward to reading his copy of “The Times” newspaper – which Wellington had luckily tidied up early that morning, out on the Common. But it was still raining just as it had been yesterday morning, and the morning before that.

“Tch tch tch,” said Great Uncle Bulgaria crossly. He stumped back into the Burrow with the newspaper crackling under his arm. It crackled because it had been very damp when Wellington found it and Madame Cholet had had to dry it out on top of her oven.

“Can’t be helped, Bulgaria,” said Tobermory. “It’s lucky we’ve got so many umbrellas in the Store Room. It’s a good thing Human Beings are forever leaving their brollies lying about. It means we’re never short of them!”

“Humph!” said Great Uncle Bulgaria. “I’m sure it never rained as much as this when I was a young Womble! We had lots and lots of sunny days.”

His study door shut with a click. Tobermory smiled to himself and then went back to looking at the rain. He was just a bit worried about the Tidying Up party who were out on the Common. All this rain had made the grass very slippery and, for another thing, there was an enormous puddle just in front of the Burrow. Even as he looked at it – it seemed to be getting bigger and bigger and BIGGER.

"Oh, they'll be all right," Tobermory said to himself. "The rain will run off their fur and the chances are they won't even notice it. You don't at their age! Still, I'll ask Madame Cholet to make an extra large helping of hot buttercup juice for when they get back!"

He needn't have worried. Tomsk, Stepney and Alderney were having a wonderful time out on the Common. Tomsk had just had a "shower" by getting the other two to shake the tree under which he was standing. Alderney had been pretending to "swim" through rain, showing off a bit as she is rather a Water Womble. She often has a paddle or a swim in the pond by her treehouse. As for Stepney – he was quite sure he could turn his wheelie barrow into a WATER wheelie barrow.

"All I've got to do," he said, "is find something in Tobermory's Workshop which I can put under the wheels…"

"What sort of something?" asked Tomsk, as they piled their full Tidy Bags onto the barrow.

"Well I dunno till I see it," said Stepney, who hadn't got the faintest idea what he was looking for exactly. But he'd think of something. He always did! "Here, lend us a paw young Wombles, this is heavy!"

It was too, because the ground was so muddy. It took all three of them to push and shove with all their might to get it up a bank. But the good part was that when they reached the top of the bank they jumped on the back and went BUMPITY BUMPITY BUMP down the other side, sending splashes of mud in all directions. In fact, they were enjoying it so much that they didn't see the now ENORMOUS puddle in front of the Burrow until it was too late.

"Yeeeee!" shouted Alderney, hanging on tight.

"Wow!" roared Tomsk.

"Whooops!" yelled Stepney. "Put the brakes on somebody…"

But it was too late!

With a great squelching, slurping sound the barrow with the three young Wombles and their Tidy Bags on the back of it went slap into the middle of the puddle. And… sank!

Luckily it didn't sink too far, only about half way up the wheels. But by the time the three of them managed to clamber down, get the Tidy Bags out and heave and push and pull the barrow into the Burrow, they were very, very muddy indeed.

"Well it can't be helped I suppose," said Great Uncle Bulgaria. "The weather really is very bad! You three had better go and have a proper wash. What are you looking so worried about, Tobermory?"

"How are we going to get in and out of the Burrow ourselves if it keeps on raining?" said Tobermory.

And it was then that Alderney, the Nearly-Water-Womble had her great idea.

"Can Tomsk and Stepney come with me to my treehouse?" she said. "Just for ten minutes? Please!"

Away they splashed with Alderney explaining as she went.

"Look!" she said as they reached the pond in front of her tree house. And there, tied to a branch among the reeds, was the raft she had made herself for collecting rubbish which had been thrown into the water. It was made of all kinds of bits and pieces, and it floated beautifully.

The three of them lifted it above their heads – apart from anything else it kept the rain off – and then they trotted back to the Burrow where everybody was waiting for them by this time. All the other Wombles stared in complete astonishment as they saw the raft coming towards them. They had never seen anything quite like it before! The three young Wombles put it down on the edge of the puddle – which was bigger than ever by this time. Then they climbed on board, picked up three paddles and rowed themselves up to the Burrow.

Great Uncle Bulgaria led the cheering.

"I tell you what," said Stepney to Alderney, "it's even better than my water wheelie barrow idea!"

"And it deserves a double helping of supper," said Great Uncle Bulgaria. "Now let's shut the front door and go into our warm, dry kitchen!"

Great Uncle Bulgaria never has a *cross*word to say. Ha ha!

But he does like to do *The Times* crossword every day.

Can you fill in the answers to this Wombling Crossword?

The answers are all things found when the Wombles tidy up Wimbledon Common!

2 Down

3 Down

4 Across

1 Across

6 Across

7 Across

4 Down

5 Down

When you've got all the answers, turn to page 61 to see if you are right.

50

SPOT the DIFFERENCE

There's nothing Orinoco likes more than picnics and lazing about on the river!

Look at these two pictures. Can you spot ten things that are different in the bottom picture?

When you think you've found the differences, turn to page 61 to see if you are right.

OBIDOS to the RESCUE

"I think," said Orinoco, "that I may just have thirty winks." But he said it in a very small voice so that Wellington, who was tidying up with him, didn't quite hear him.

"Sorry. What? Yes, all right," said Wellington. "I'll take the left-hand path. See you later then…"

"Much later," said Orinoco in an even smaller voice. It was a lovely warm day and he was really quite tired after tidying up two cans of fizzy lemonade, two small cushions, and a piece of bendy wire. All he needed was one more thing and his Tidy Bag would be quite full.

Orinoco gave a happy sigh, found a nice quiet bush and got ready to settle down. All the Wombles were a bit tired this morning because Cairngorm the MacWomble was visiting them from his burrow near Loch Ness in Scotland, and he had made them all dance the MacWomble jig after supper.

"Cushion's not quite big enough," Orinoco mumbled to himself, as he tried to arrange one under his back paws and one under his head. But this must really have been his lucky day because at that moment he spotted just what he wanted right underneath the bush. It was a soft-looking brown paper parcel. Orinoco pulled it out, gave a happy sigh and settled his sleepy head on it. But only for about half a second, because he hadn't so much as given half a snore, when the parcel made the most awful moaning sound right in his ear. For such a fat, round Womble, Orinoco moved very fast indeed. One moment he was lying down and the next he was on the other side of the bush with one eye looking round it.

The parcel slowly straightened out and gave another dreadful groan.

This time it was so loud that Wellington heard it and came running up.

"What-what-what was that?" whispered Wellington.

"That-that-that," said Orinoco, pointing one shaky paw, and as he did the parcel uncreased itself and gave a third fur-tingling moan.

The two young Wombles stayed absolutely still, holding onto each other, but nothing else happened.

"We-we'd better take it back to Tobermory," whispered Wellington. "He'll know what to do with it."

"I hope it doesn't get out and bite us," said Orinoco as they tiptoed back to the Burrow.

But when they got there the Workshop was empty except for cousin Obidos from Brazil. He was whistling away to himself as he worked because he was trying to keep his spirits up. He was feeling a bit homesick this morning because suddenly Wimbledon seemed a very long way from Brazil.

"What you got there?" he asked.

Wellington and Orinoco put the Thing down very gently on the floor and told Obidos all about it.

"It's some dreadful, awful creature that groans..." said Orinoco.

"I think it's a flying parcel from outer space," said Wellington.

"Hmm," said Obidos.

He could see that the other two were quite scared, so that made him feel quite brave. He would show them what Brazilian Wombles were made of!

"We get all kinds of strange creatures in my country," he said, and he stepped forward and undid the parcel. It gave one very small wail and then as the paper came away the three of them found themselves looking at a kind of brightly coloured bundle with pipes sticking out of it. All three of them stared at it for a moment and then Obidos clapped his paws together and darted over to one of the Workshop shelves. He picked up a small set of pipes, took a deep breath and began to blow. The pipes made a wonderful flute-like kind of music which carried right through the Burrow. It really was a magical sound.

"You see," said Obidos, pausing for breath. "These are my pipes from Brazil and that – that creature there is a bagging pipe from Scotland. Try it and see!"

"Rather," said Wellington, who wanted to make the same kind of magic music as Obidos. He picked up the pipes, took a deep breath and blew. The noise was truly awful. It too travelled right through the Burrow.

Some Wombles fled for cover, others bolted out of the front door and Great Uncle Bulgaria, who had been talking to Cairngorm in his study, put his paws over his ears and bellowed: "STOP THAT AT ONCE!"

"The pipes, the bonny pipes!" said Cairngorm. "Och I must away and play them. But properly!"

"I was afraid you'd say that," said Great Uncle Bulgaria, but Cairngorm was already striding towards the Workshop.

It was some time later that Tobermory returned to the Burrow to find the Wimbledon Wombles with their eyes shut and their front paws stuffed in their ears.

"What a din!" said Tobermory. "If I'm not mistaken, Cairngorm's got hold of some bagpipes… we'll have to get him out on the Common…"

"Tobermory, do something," said Great Uncle Bulgaria.

In the Workshop, Cairngorm and Obidos were marching round and round playing their pipes and having a wonderful time, while Orinoco and Wellington were beating time with spoons on tin plates. They seemed to be enjoying it too.

"Outside," said Tobermory, holding the door open and showing them the way. Out marched the band, down the passage, out through the front door and onto the Common which, luckily, was deserted so early in the morning.

"I can still hear them," groaned Great Uncle Bulgaria.

Tobermory said "tch tch tch," picked up Orinoco's Tidy Bag and took out the two small cushions, and the piece of bendy wire, and in two seconds he had made Great Uncle Bulgaria a beautiful pair of soundproof earmuffs.

Peace descended on the Burrow while out on the Common the four-piece Brazilian Womble Band were having the time of their lives.

THE TIMES

WHAT a RACKET!

Can you remember who played which instrument? Draw a line to join each Womble to their favourite way of making noise!

Cairngorm

Orinoco

Wellington

Obidos

Make a MEGAPHONE

"That was lots of fun! If you follow these instructions you can make a megaphone and make lots of noise too."

You will need:
One piece of A4 white paper
Safety scissors
Sticky tape
A plastic yoghurt pot

1 Cut two oblongs from the side of a plastic yoghurt pot.

2 Put the oblongs together, so they curve towards one another. Then stick them together with sticky tape. This is your mouthpiece.

3 Take your piece of paper and roll it into a cone. Where the paper overlaps, fasten it together with sticky tape.

4 Ask an adult to cut off the narrow end of the cone.

5 Push the mouthpiece into the hole in the end of the cone. Stick the cone and the mouthpiece together with sticky tape.

To use your megaphone hold it to your mouth and talk into the mouthpiece. You can decorate your megaphone using coloured pencils.

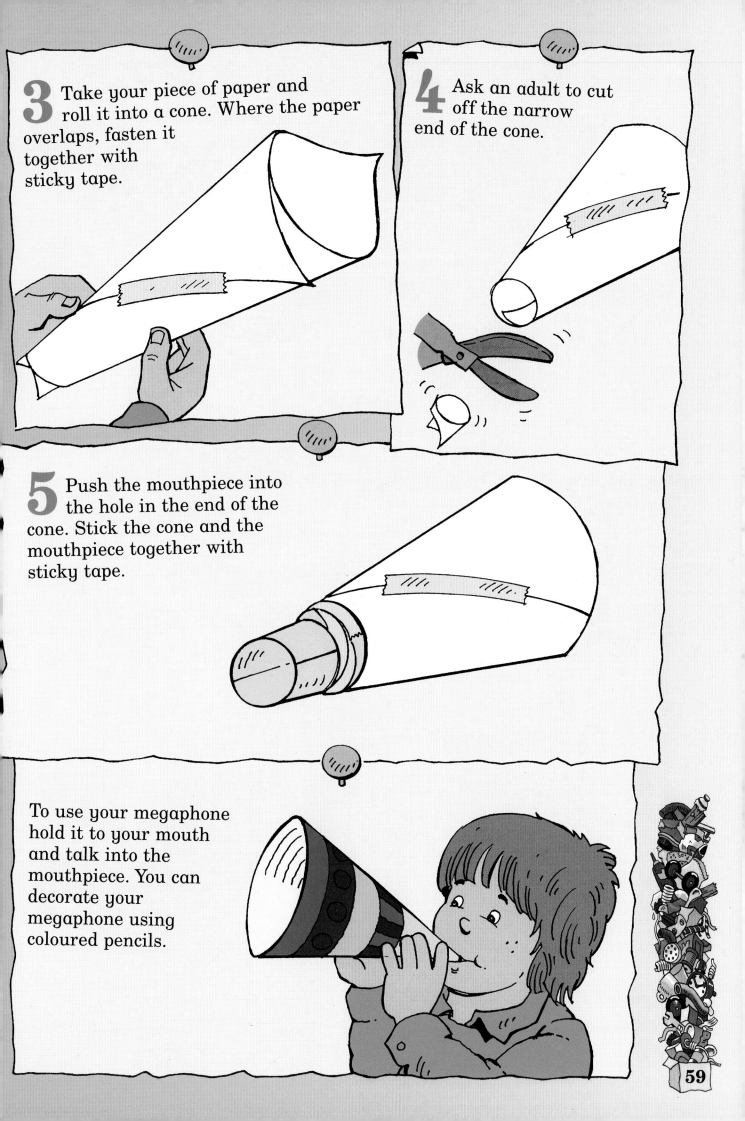

Orinoco's Day

Answers

Page 24

T	O	M	S	K	C	V	A
G	W	N	H	Q	Z	X	L
M	O	E	A	E	L	M	D
W	B	U	N	G	O	O	E
N	I	K	S	K	I	U	R
Z	D	C	I	B	T	W	N
H	O	M	E	R	Q	P	E
N	S	T	E	P	N	E	Y

Page 50

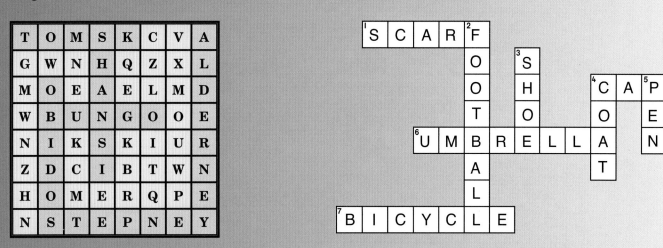

Page 51

61